The shelf is filled with records.

I walk over to pick one at random from the bunch.
Arcade *by Tomppabeats.*

Scratches heard by starting the record player
are overruled by a layer of crackle on the audio
of track one.

The room is filled with a Spanish sample, Tanto Amor.

It is late at night, a seemingly forgotten hour according
to society.

I keep rewinding the record until dawn.

Longing for Lo-fi

Glimpsing back through technology

Sébastien Bovie

Contents

Preface

The small lamp on my desk illuminates
my notes and books with a slightly yellow hue.
The window is open and a small breeze promenades
through the room. I am surrounded by an imaginary
miniature city that has skyscrapers composed out
of books. Lo-fi hip hop is playing softly through
the speakers of my laptop, accompanied by rain
added to the track from another open tab. It is 2 a.m.,
I close the text document in which I am writing.
An internet browser pops up, showing a moody Bart
Simpson driving on what seems like an endless road.
It is looped and I am now looking at the tiny canyon-
like spaces between the books on my desk, imagining
Bart cruising around in a miniature car.

The YouTube track is called S O U L
S E A R C H I N G [2] by Neotic. Looking at this,
Bart seemed unsuccessful in the search for his soul.
The spacing between the letters even go so far
as to suggest the letters are searching for each other,
just like us, searching for ourselves in the forsaken
hours late at night. I truly hope Bart ends up
finding his soul, yet as I scroll through the sidebar
of YouTube's algorithmic suggestions, I notice a new
video that is a sequel to this one. His now more than
two hour directionless drive exists to support others'
searching, or as I was doing, working.

Bart's eyes are heavy and his slow blinking
is contagious. It does not take long before I become
aware of my own tired eyes. Besides the fairly
muffled beats on the track, there is hardly any
noise. Outside cars pass by, I guess complete silence
has become nearly extinct in cities anyway. Not sure
if these cars can be considered noise, as it feels like
they exist as an extension of the track. I could
say that these drivers outside pass by Bart
in an opposite direction.

I close my laptop and the music halts.
As I drift to my bed, the sound of the wooden floor
resembles the crackle experience that is digitally
added to lo-fi tracks, as if it is still playing through
my speakers. The moment right before I fall asleep,
I imagine Bart Simpson pulling over and dozing off
too, because it seems we are both exhausted.

To some people this will be a familiar feeling,
while to others, it might seem like an entirely new
take on this kind of music and perhaps even far-
fetched. In this essay, I will elaborate on a couple
of viewpoints on the topic of lo-fi music.

There are people who listen to lo-fi
and experience a longing for a different time,
while others just long for focus. A big part of lo-fi
is the sentiment of nostalgia. Lo-fi uses this nostalgic
longing to construct a desiring mood for a time
passed. Aside from the focus on lo-fi and its use
of nostalgia, these texts will elaborate on the relation
between lo-fi and the capitalist society of today.
Analysing the accompanying images will further
support these characteristics that prove vital
to the genre.

All chapters are built on essential pillars
of philosophical theory, but do not let this discourage
you. I have researched their connection to lo-fi
(at least how I find them relevant) as well as I can,
and I can only hope that this might end up being
a stepping stone for you, the reader, to take
a moment and reflect on both lo-fi and society.

As for this book, it started with a long thought process about how this music genre is perceived by different people. I have to thank my friends and internet strangers for discussing their reasons for listening to lo-fi hip hop. I must stress that I am not an academic in music studies, nor in psychology or anthropology. *Longing for Lo-fi* is my attempt to frame this music genre. I am merely connecting some of the dots between critical thinkers and lo-fi music, and maybe you, the reader, can keep connecting them further.

SOUL SEARCHING²
Neotic — 31 august 2020

Life distorded

These days, my YouTube recommendations are filled with cartoon imagery from the 90s, combined with moody titles. Writing *Longing for Lo-fi* is obviously often accompanied by that genre playing in the background. Over time, I have become a method actor, as my YouTube algorithm has undergone a metamorphosis. My homepage now feels like my childhood living room after 4 p.m., where we came home to as kids and put on our favourite tv-shows. We threw our books into a corner of the room and discarded our dirty shoes by the door to avoid remarks about messing up the carpet. Time froze as we resided in a mental cocoon. Why is it that lo-fi music creates a longing for being a kid in the 90s?

In the upcoming part, we will think about what nostalgia is and how a psychological aspect to this 'moody' genre is present in lo-fi hip hop. I do wish to state that there is no need, as a listener, to actually experience this side of the music and aesthetic. I can imagine people listening to it simply because they like the downbeat tempo and relaxing vibes this genre radiates.

*Glimpsing
back through
technology*

You're in Hey Arnold's room in 1997 listening to music and it's raining | 3 HOUR ASMR Ambience
Kitspy's Dreamland — 28 june 2021

It's late at night. Every now and then, a lonely car drives by in the street below my window. The faint noise of tires on a wet road sounds like soothing white noise. I am reminded of how the world goes on, despite my efforts to stay up late. To stay awake until that specific moment where time seems to halt. A GIF from Hey Arnold *fills my monitor screen as I am writing some notes down on paper.*

I always thought Arnold's bedroom was amazing, with the large skylight and elevated sleeping area. You're in Hey Arnold's room in 1997 listening to music and it's raining, *the title of the YouTube video isn't lying and transports me through time and space.*

First off, there are some typical, technical characteristics that distinguishes lo-fi from the other side of the spectrum, hi-fi. High-fidelity is the term for sound recordings that aspire to a pristine reproduction of the original performance of the audio. The medium of recording is rendered transparent through noise reduction and other strategies of purification. We have come to a point where this (re-)production quality has almost reached technical perfection. High-fidelity sound recording has been debunked as an idealised impossibility. Present-day technology has challenged and succeeded in creating audio quality so high, it is as if it were a live performance. Although this does not fool us the way one might assume. The extremely high quality of the audio does not remove our awareness of the fact that it represents something it is not. Although we experience the recording as the original, we are aware we are being tricked, for it stays a representation of the real. However, listeners of hi-fi recordings desire to be wrapped in this suggestion, they want to fully emerge themselves in sound only.

He concludes with: It puts the machines into a category where machines probably belong— colourful, buzzing, cuddly things with the lifespan of hamsters. My Powerbook has the lifespan of a hamster. Exactly how attached can I become to this machine? Just how much of an emotional investment can I make in my beloved three-thousand- dollar hamster?

[...]

An Olympian pity rules. We are as gods to our mere mortal media—we kill them for our sport.

'The life and death of media' in Sound Unbound, Bruce Sterling (2008), p. 76.

Side A

In a short essay in *Sound Unbound*, Bruce Sterling writes about 'dead media' and what this implies. In an age of such high-quality reproduction of audio as well as video, we have to reassess our position to the media and the now many reproductions and images that flood our daily lives. There are many forms of media that are threatened to become obsolete e.g. the book or cinema, with the introduction of bigger and better televisions. Yet, Sterling notes that something has changed in the progress of technology; present-day media and gadgets exist in planned obsolescence. What he means is that new gadgets often result in being outdated once they are released onto the market and end up as tomorrow's waste. We might even say that, rather than becoming obsolete, they are killed.

As we are unstoppably evolving in the digital space and age, we mourn the lost and seemingly more authentic media. To mourn might be a heavy word, but it is an aura that is created by old media aids while constructing a new universe of watching, listening and overall experiencing. Besides the desire for authentic forms of media like a book, one might also state that older media was made with less of a consumerist mindset. Where in the past older forms of media were built to last, like books and radios, nowadays they are built to be consumed and then disposed of. Analogue longing is not necessarily about a protest against digital technologies evolving at high pace, but about applying that digital remediation of analogue aesthetics within the digital environment to appease our dead-media-longing. Being confronted with this aspect of dead media, we have an impression that we rediscovered something lost, right before it would have completely disappeared.

It would not be an overstatement to say
that this lo-fi genre is a form of auditory escapism,
this subtle immersion of sound could be a form
of escape from the daily routine that is life. It should
be no surprise that hi-fi listening was desirable
in the earlier time frame of music development
and production, when society was still in its Fordist
period (on which later we will continue).

What happens in lo-fi music?
There is no aspiration to seclude the music
and listen to it by itself, as is happening in hi-fi.
Our current age is defined by post-Fordist
capitalism, a system that has evolved from mass-
production of the same thing (Fordism) to small
and precise manufacturing processes and services
that support the growing individualism. This comes
with a bigger workload, more responsibilities
for the employer, undefined working hours, endless
streams of e-mails... In this post-Fordist era, noise
and social life are ever-present. People listening
to lo-fi hip hop often approach this from a stance
of beats to relax to/beats to study to/beats to sleep
to, as these titles often encourage you to.
As opposed to hi-fi, lo-fi has the ability to be
looped in the background and integrate itself
with common-day noise. That aspect of lo-fi
is essential in understanding why lo-fi is so desired
by the younger generations of today. They are
aware of the constant lurking pressure raised
by globalised capitalism. They are capitalist realists.
There is an awareness of their inevitability to halt
the world, so they escape into this moment of music.

Crackled

Side A

An essential technique in this genre
is the crackle. These tracks are obviously some
sort of simulation playing in a nostalgic mode.
When we listen to them for the first time,
the digitally added effects will create a vibe which
allows reminiscing, along with added nostalgic
samples we might use to create a context of longing.
We can listen to something that has only been
released in the past month, yet have the feeling
that it has always existed and have often heard
it in our childhood.

The crackle is quintessential for the genre
of lo-fi culture. This might correlate with music
fans now also being fascinated by older playback
technologies like vinyl, audiotaping and so on.
'Dead media,' as Sterling mentioned. The fixation
on this material might also be why lo-fi adopted
the crackle to its genre. Hearing the crackle
in the audio makes us aware that we are listening
to a time that is non-present. Sample tunes are now
drenched in so much crackle, reverb and underlying
beats per minute that they dissolve into a suggestive
audio-fog. The cracks are reduced to subtle hints,
like nudges to the past. The noise obstructs us from
fully engaging with the musical layer of the track.
It is similar to the obstruction experienced in
engaging with our environment in day-to-day life.
"Crackle makes us aware that we are hearing
a recording but also makes us think about the
playback systems we use to access the recordings,"
according to Ian Penman, British writer and music
journalist for the magazines Uncut, The Wire,
The Guardian, and explicitly referred to as
an inspiration to writers like Simon Reynolds
and Mark Fisher..

This layer of crackling might get its pleasing nature from nostalgic references, but it also asks the listeners to actually consider the nature of production.

Crackle ends up being a tool used for a certain sense of historical vibes, but it also manages to create a kind of fantastic past. Crackle in lo-fi now functions not only as a throwback, but as a comfort zone of soft, soothing white noise. This opposes the asocial, individualistic society. A place where a small-child utopia lives on in the fog of the crackle and reverb beats.

SIDE A
Track 03

*My head,
somewhere else*

I recently rewatched Avatar: The Last Airbender.

I get why a kid attempted to escape from carrying
the weight of responsibility on his shoulders.
Many characters are troubled due to trauma
and destiny, they are conflicted. Certain quotes feel
like a punch in the gut, especially now that I am older.

Yet I often catch myself wondering what they talk
about in the liminal spaces of travel. The hours
they spend on a flying bison, on a ship and so on...
Pondering a life without the weight of their
responsibility? Without the inevitability
of their destiny?

What does that small-child utopia consist of and how is it enforced, besides that drone-like crackle? Besides the obvious crackle, we are confronted with an unlimited amount of samples in tracks that date back to different eras. Because of the internet, anything that would have been lost in the past can never be actually lost. The most niche episodes of a 70s show can be found online on YouTube, giving music producers the possibility to implement these into lo-fi tracks. When listening to these tracks, one is often met with specific, borrowed samples at the beginning of the track. This allows for an immediate mood. This mood shrouds the entire track with nostalgia. The sample is often accompanied by an underlying or veiled (so to speak) melody of the show.

These samples are not necessary, but we see that using them leads to conversations in the comment sections of these YouTube videos regarding the character, the quote and so on and can thus be seen as an invitation for the community to discuss the sample. It often is a supportive or inspirational sample, that adds to the already supportive community giving space for people to share in the comment section what weighs on their hearts.

An obvious example is 1HR Uncle Iroh Inspiration - Avatar Lofi Study Beats by Olivia Tataro on YouTube. This playlist has multiple tracks, often separated by a voice track of what Uncle Iroh might say. Uncle Iroh, a character from Avatar: The Last Airbender and The Legend of Korra, has this parental wisdom and a care-free attitude towards major events, time, family, etc. These samples can throw us back into a non-time, where we can still use Iroh's paternal wisdom, as it is often a mindful way of thinking, for example:

You sound like my nephew, always thinking you need to do things on your own without anyone's support. There is nothing wrong with letting people who love you, help you.

The Chase
AVATAR: THE
LAST AIRBENDER,
Book 2 ep. 8
(2006).

This is a sample from *Avatar: the Last Airbender*, which aired in 2006. One of the interesting things about lo-fi hip hop is that the samples used are never explicitly stated in the description. Despite this, many of its listeners are aware of its provenance, its origin. We can often trace the origin of the sample through discussions or memories that are brought up in the comment sections of the tracks, even if there are no explicit credits.

The adaptation of the melody and the samples returns this to the more mechanical and seemingly outdated age of listening to music. With this form comes another aspect of nostalgic feeling. The nostalgic feeling of analog listening, similar to crackle, where the texture of sound creates an extra dimension. Yet this analog form has a dual function. Semiotically, this analog listening in our present-day operates at the 'indexical' level. An index of this kind has special potential for creating direct emotional effects when tied to personal memories such as those from childhood because they are perceived as 'real' or 'true'. In that sense, parts of the experiences get signified. We hear Uncle Iroh now, yet we are brought back to our childhood sitting in front of the television and listening to his words.

Although, his wisdom hits different as we have gained a broader life experience. It is this sensation of familiarity or of well-being that would imply the maternal body, according to Freud on the topic

of déjà vu. Although this feeling is based on
an illusion, it is still valuable. Following this idea
of Freud's desire for the maternal womb, I wish
to nuance this. I do not think that we desire
the womb anymore, but these lo-fi samples
evoke a form of appeal to us in a specific way.
A way of reliving a time without worries, a way
of substituting our daily life for a time of less
responsibility. Experiencing a time where one was
almost without responsibility and being taken care
of by a father and mother-role. Although this peering
into the past through the medium of lo-fi is personal
and even partly fictional, it is nevertheless bound
up with reality and individually lived experience(s),
brought back through these samples in the music.

*Don't want
the lie to end*

SICKNESS
UNTO DEATH,
Soren
Kierkegaard
(1849),
p. 176-177.

The dog kennel by the palace

*To what shall we compare the relation between
the thinker's system and his actual existence?*

*A thinker erects this immense building, a system,
a system which embraces the whole existence
and world history etc.— and if we contemplate
his personal life, we discover to our astonishment
this terrible and ludicrous fact, that he himself
personally does not live in this immense high-vaulted
place, but in a barn alongside it, or in a dog kennel,
or at most in the porter's lodge.*

*If one were to take the liberty of calling his attention
to this by a single word, he would be offended.
For he has no fear of being under a delusion,
if only he can get the system completed.....
By means of the delusion.*

Yet when thinking about it, we are completely
aware that we are being conned. Even though
our brain constructs this homely feeling, this longing
in the music is fairly explicit because of the crackle,
samples and nostalgic imagery. However, the other
side of this dual function seeps through more subtly.
Besides the fact that lo-fi hip hop is a contemporary
music genre, sampling old cartoons and tv-shows,
there are many more facets that make us aware
that there are different kinds of feelings at play.
Discrepancies in texture applied through digital
tools mean that they do not belong to the past,
nor the present. As mentioned before, we are aware
that sampling doesn't make sense in the technical
ageing-process. The sample exists in a liminal
context. To the listener the samples are not
of the present, but also not entirely historical.

The samples exist in a limbo due to the current-day platforms on which they are being listened to and the technological improvements of the ageing-effects and so on.

The tracks now exist in a universe that is 'void' of time. A universe that plays into our childhood memories, where we yearn for the past, a past with fewer worries, but also a time that never existed so explicitly. A feeling that is well captured in 'hauntology', a term applied by British philosophy and radical politics writer Mark Fisher whose ideas often find their way through subjects of popular culture and music. 'Hauntology' is a term now used by critics in reference to paradoxes found in postmodernity, specifically the recurring usage of retro aesthetics and the impossibility to escape old social forms.

'Nostalgia mode' is a term coined by Frederic Jameson, Marxist and philosopher who was a key-influence on Fisher's writing. This term focuses on the historical aspect of nostalgia where one might use tools and techniques in a different way. For the above-mentioned tools (like crackle) are a necessity, yet this Nostalgia-mode of Jameson's is valuable as it connects the psychological part and mechanical part as two aspects of one mode. This counters the common approach that views the experience of the listener as a different field of study than the study of mechanical evolution, disconnecting mediums and users from each other. Jameson addresses this with a couple of examples, but the most interesting one to me is one from *Star Wars*, where he mentions:

'Postmodernism and Consumer Society' in THE CULTURAL TURN: SELECTED WRITINGS ON THE POSTMODERN 1983-1998, p. 8.

One of the most important cultural experiences of the generations that grew up from the 1930s to the 1950s was the Saturday afternoon series of the Buck Rogers type — alien villains, true American heroes, heroines in distress, the death ray or the doomsday box, and the cliff-hanger at the end whose miraculous solution was to be witnessed next Saturday afternoon. Star Wars reinvented this experience in the form of a pastiche; there is no point to a parody of such a series, since they are long extinct. Far from being a pointless satire of such dead forms, Star Wars satisfies a deep longing to experience them again; it is a complex object in which on some first level children and adolescents can take the adventures straight, while the adult public is able to gratify a deeper and more properly nostalgic desire to return to that older period and to live it's strange old aesthetic artefacts through once again.

To bring this example into the present, we could say that we now no longer want to bring back the Buck Rogers type sci-fi that dominated television pre-60s. What we see is a longing for the older *Star Wars* movies. *The Mandalorian* is a current-day TV series made for the Disney+ streaming service set in the universe of *Star Wars*. This is a great example of this booming trend as it builds on that 'nostalgia mode', with characters and places like in the older *Star Wars* movies, the use of real costumes and props over CGI, scenes on location... Not just with *Star Wars*, but with many other universes and genres, we see the longing for a time that has passed. Yet can we say it is just the past that we yearn for? There is no longing for that specific historical period, no longing for a date or year but a longing that is a yearning to form. In *Ghosts of my Life*, Mark Fisher works with the idea that we prefer these

nostalgic ghosts, as they still hold that aura
of a possibly brighter future. If we take
the case of *Star Wars*, we can project it onto
lo-fi in an interesting way. To some, lo-fi is a nice
downbeat track to work or relax to, while to others,
it will be associated with a memory that can
be appreciated by those who lived in the same
time period as the sample. When listening
to the mandalorion - lo-fi by Closed on Sunday,
we are in the same *Star Wars*-universe that Jameson
brought up. The artificial ageing of the sample,
places it in that aforementioned 'void' of time.
The listener is aware that they are listening
to an aged version of a contemporary track.
Those who watch the show are aware that it
has only just aired, yet due to the technical tools
that place the music in a void they find themselves
in a vague state of a mental past. The nostalgia
that this present-day track brings on is coined
as 'Reflective Nostalgia' by Svetlana Boym,
a Russian-American writer and media artist
that explored topics such as modernity and memory,
homesickness and utopias. Reflective nostalgia
cherishes those shattered fragments of memory.
Emma Winston elaborates on this in her academic
article *Beats to Relax/Study To: Contradiction
and Paradox in Lofi Hip Hop*. Winston suggests
that the online context where lo-fi exists, "makes
the bric-a-brac of nostalgia available in digital
form, appearing more desirable than the real
artefact." This is also the case for other nostalgia-
ruled genres like synthwave and vaporwave.
We are aware of the artificiality, yet we prefer
the illusion that comes with this nostalgia.
This can also be found in the comments,
where people write out small stories of fiction
that create a context.

the mandalorian - lofi
Closed on Sunday — 2 november 2020

Freud implied that when we look back
on our memories we fill in gaps, and that this
is an essential piece of what makes us human.
Simply the samples of children's cartoons are enough
to recall our childhoods. There is no need to have
seen that actual cartoon, or to know what episode
the sample has come from; the 'nostalgia mode'
is enough to recollect the general time-period.
We are willing to fully emerge ourselves
in a time that actually never occurred.

2049
implemented
memories

Blade Runner 2049 is an interesting case study concerning this aspect of memory. It is a science-fiction movie directed by Denis Villeneuve, also known for his movies *Dune and Arrival*. The main character, K, is artificial, born of technology. He is a law enforcing replicant, a humanoid robot tasked to hunt down older versions of his kind... a blade runner. The movie has underlying concepts of the value of memory, forming an identity and a quest for the distinctly human. Although the aesthetics of this movie lean more towards the music genre of synthwave and cyberpunk, where a science-fiction dystopian society rules over the masses, it is still applicable to the case of our longing for lo-fi. Not only from the fact that *Blade Runner 2049* is a sequel of the cult-classic *Blade Runner*, similar to the *Star Wars*-franchise and its resurfacing, but the societal construction of the movie serves the purpose of highlighting the idea of lo-fi. Connecting this science-fiction noir setting to our seemingly wholesome lo-fi genre, we have to elaborate on another term: 'Hauntology.' Addressed in Fisher's writings, hauntology shows a longing for lost futures where utopia is still an opportunity. *Blade Runner 2049* draws this dystopia even further away from the present feeling that 'hauntology' already has. The movie does this by introducing dystopian concepts such as artificial intelligence as romantic partners, preconstructed and artificially induced memories of a time long lost serving purpose as a mental escape and a god-like individual obsessed with the idea of creation. In 2023, some people are already living in their past, pondering plausible, alternative future timelines over the everyday worries they now have, hoping for another society. Yet, in *Blade Runner 2049*, this longing seems even harder to reach

as that society crumbled further into dystopia.
The possibility to think back to a specific moment
where we could go in a different direction
as a society is now long gone.

The idea of memory implants and memory
engineers is the focus of this case-study, the movie
addresses an interesting detail of the main
character's (who is a replicant) memory. K
(later on called Joe) goes through a personality
development, a hero's journey, creating his own
individuality. This is possible through the idea that
this replicant, who at first seems to have no free will,
encounters an older type of his kind elaborating
on the miracle of the possibility of non-human birth.
Connecting this to a memory K seems to relive over
and over again and the confirmation of his consumer
product romantic partner, who is a hologram, K now
redefines himself as the 'chosen one.' In his quest
for his origin, he seeks the creator of his artificially
induced childhood memory.

K meets with a memory engineer called Ana
Stelline, who can be found engineering memories
in a dome. The dome protects her from the outside
hazards of the world as she suffers from a compro-
mised immune system. "A life of freedom, as long
as it is behind glass," she mentions to K. Interestingly,
she does not feel that the dome limits her freedom.
She lives in this world of creating and engineering
fictional memories for others, shrouded from what
happens outside, what the dystopian world is going
through. Whilst working, she resides in those
Freudian gaps of memory she creates so well.
K mentions she is the best memory-maker there
is, where she replies that her use comes in with
humanity needing a stable product. With a stable

50

Side A

product, she refers to these replicants who can only function with a form of escape, a memory to escape from the grim present of their endless exploitation. Before this implementation, replicants rebelled against the humans that were using them as tireless labour machines. Ana's ideology of engineering memories opposes the notion of repressing the replicants through fictional escape, her ideology is one of compassion:

> *Ana: I think it's only kind. Replicants live such hard lives, made to do what we'd rather not. I can't help your future... But I can give you good memories to think back on and smile.*
>
> *K: It's nice.*
>
> *Ana: It's better than nice. It feels authentic. And if you have authentic memories, you have real human responses.*
>
> *K: Are they all constructed or do you ever use ones that are real?*
>
> *Ana: It's illegal to use real memories, officer.*
>
> *K: How can you tell the difference? Can you tell if something... really happened?*
>
> *Ana: They all think it's about more details. But that is not how memory works. We recall with our feelings. Anything real should be a mess.*

With this dialogue, we see a clear connection between the idea of fictional memories and how glimpsing back, even though they are fictional, can be a form of consolation. Its relevance to current day developments is also closer than one might think, although saying we are close to the dystopian context of *Blade Runner 2049* might be too extreme. Ana implements memories that make life easier and more bearable for the constructs (replicants) who do the tedious chores in the dystopian community. Living in an even more polarised world, in this case humans against robots created in a humanoid manner, these replicants are repressed in such a way that their recollection of an innocent past is their way of escapism. Listening to lo-fi and hearing those tunes from childhood are not that much different from K focusing on the one memory he has. There is truth to his memory even though it is implemented, yet it is not completely his truth.Someone lived it, but not him specifically. This does not take away his comfort of that memory and even influences, towards the peak of the movie, his decision making. Just as K values his non-lived memory, we value our reflective nostalgia and the possibility to escape into that construct, away from our day-to-day worries.

*looking back,
finding gaps*

SOUL SEARCHING [3]
Neotic — 21 march 2021

Nostalgia and casting our eyes to our past
is intrinsically human. Who doesn't get lost
in hypotheses of the past? It would not be such
a widely covered topic or emotion in literature,
if it wasn't as inevitable as it is human. I catch
myself zoning out in the passenger seat, eyes staring
blankly at the meadows accompanying the highway.
This is probably that SOUL SEARCHING
that Bart is going through. We're glimpsing back
and trying to experience our past.

In the end, the nostalgic sentiment is caused by memories resurfacing and glimpses into the past. What are nostalgia, melancholy and mourning — three terms that might be inherently connected to lo-fi? They are emotional states that occur when looking back at the past. These states are a necessity when it comes to addressing the past, according to Walter Benjamin, the Frankfurter Schule philosopher and critical theorist who lived in the first half of the 20th century. He writes:

Language has unmistakably made plain that memory is not an instrument for exploring the past, but rather a medium. It is the medium of that which is experienced, just as earth is the medium in which ancient cities lie buried. [...]

ILLUMINATIONS (III.), Walter Benjamin, p. 179 1968.

And in a following writing on *Eingedenken* (remembrance) and *Erfahrung* (experience), he clarifies:

Erfahrung is defined less as the "product of facts firmly anchored in memory than of a convergence in memory of accumulated and frequently unconscious data."

Ibid.

This is essential for the bond between experience and remembrance. Unconscious is key in the sentence on *Erfahrung*. Benjamin ventures into psychoanalysis with a notion of the vague collection of memories instead of concrete and defining moments. As previously addressed when Freud was brought up: Benjamin's statement should not seem far-fetched. Benjamin points to Freud's insight, that memory fragments are often most potent when the process that left them behind never became conscious. In relation to lo-fi, this would

mean that we do not need the exact details
that go with the moment of the past.
This comes back to Svetlana Boym's 'Reflective
Nostalgia', which differs a bit from psychoanalysis.
Boym's 'Reflective Nostalgia' counters psychoanalysis' statement, where it is stated that even
in an unconscious state we are fully aware
of how those past moments felt, while Boym
would say the entire happening of reminiscing
on past happenings is occurring in a fictional
world. Freud continues: "Instead of producing
a memory, the event is unconsciously repeated
in action over and over again." The suggestion
brought forward here subverts the common
opposition of remembering/forgetting and points
to the persistence of those forgotten memories.

Walter Benjamin goes on to write about Franz
Kafka, who is an influential modernist writer
best known for his works *The Metamorphosis*
and *The Castle*. Benjamin stresses a specific notion
of Kafka's work that: "The fact that it is now
forgotten does not mean that it does not extend into
the present. On the contrary: it is actually by virtue
of this very oblivion." The feelings we endured are
stronger than the concrete emotions. We might not
remember all the mundane day-to-day details, only
if these are associated with irregularity. The large
stack of vague happenings that we carry with us
in our subconscious memory has more impact
than a concrete memory.

This is what might be the appeal: the nostalgic
aspect of lo-fi. Memories are essential, as memory
engineers in *Blade Runner 2049* would acknowledge.
The underlying emotions that go with them such
as nostalgia, melancholy and mourning are often

unnoticed, but might be there nonetheless even if we do not experience them explicitly. This psychoanalysation of the genre might seem somewhat excessive, but it is important to stay critical and think about why different aspects that rule lo-fi hip hop have started spreading towards mainstream pop-culture.

*Micro-fictions —
YouTube poetry*

BERLIN
CHILDHOOD
(revised
in 1938), Walter
Benjamin, 2006.

*In 1932, when I was abroad, it began to be clear
to me that I would soon have to bid a long, perhaps
lasting farewell to the birth of my city. Several times
in my inner life, I had already experienced the process
of inoculation as something salutary. In this situation,
too, I resolved to follow this suit, and I deliberately
called to mind those images which, in exile, are most
apt to waken homesickness: images of childhood.
My assumption was that the feeling of longing would
no more gain mastery over my spirit than a vaccine
does over a healthy body. I sought to limit its effect
through insight into the irretrievability—not
the contingent biographical but the necessary social
irretrievability—of the past.This has meant that
certain biographical features, which stand out
more readily in the continuity of experience
than in its depths, altogether recede in the present
undertaking. [...]*

*But, then, the images of my metropolitan childhood
perhaps are capable, at their core, of pre-forming
later historical experience.*

Walter Benjamin wrote this as an introduction
to his *Berlin Childhood* (revised in 1938) essays.
Later in the essays, he writes about his childhood
memories of Berlin in the early 1900s. Berlin,
at that time, was flourishing with its industry
and revolutionary technology. Yet he writes
about specific memories in a vague timeframe,
not the impactful historical events. As a child,
he wandered through the cityscape carelessly
and noticed details like a clothesline running
from a loggia to a lone palm tree.

When he glimpses back to an irretrievable memory, reminding himself of the fact of irretrievability, he looks back with a certain contained longing. He knows his Berlin is not the same anymore, not only due to political context, but also because of the ever-changing society and the yearning for progression. He longs for a slower time, a time opposed to progress. A time where a kid would have the entire afternoon to play or watch stuff.

It is not just an assumption that people listening to lo-fi experience it as moody or nostalgic. Benjamin disciplined himself by remembering that those times are, in a way, past—although reminiscing brings back the moment to the present. Lo-fi music as a medium holds the possibility of disciplining us in a similar manner. One where we look back in time through the medium of the music genre.

A peculiar thing happens in the comment sections on YouTube. This reminiscing does not only remain introspective. It is interesting that these personal experiences of this reflective nostalgia are shared in these comments through the form of creative writing that is a transparent fictionalisation of an imaginary past. This past, which exists in a void, is a place where the community writes these emotional, narrative micro-fictions in response to the track or playlist. This means that the comment section becomes a combination of discussion on the samples used — which aids Boym's point of view on the ambiguity of nostalgia — and these 'micro-fictions', a term adapted by Emma Winston in *Beats to Relax/Study: Contradiction and Paradox in Lofi Hip Hop to* that refers to the small writing prompts that are explicitly creating a scene that aids in this collective nostalgic recollection. Through the juxtaposition of these two, it creates a space where you have the personal, emotional connections right next to fictionalisations and an imaginary past. As Winston elaborates: "They are, so to say, consumed adjacent to each other and are equally worthy."

As the discussion about samples of the past and fictional writing prompts interoperate, the listener (aware of the impossibility of a sample track in a past time) will be aided in reflective nostalgia through a small writing prompt described in the comment section. These two colliding shows that: if a longing exists for something that can never be retrieved, lo-fi hip hop is an elaboration on that tendency. Not only is the nostalgic object acknowledged and cherished for its irretrievability, but also for the very fact that it was never experienced in the first place.

It doesn't matter if comments and samples are connected to actual events or complete fiction, either way they have the same impact on the people reading the comments. People engulf themselves in the emotional state of nostalgia and are often supportive and wholesome about it to one another. The titles of the YouTube videos add to this effect too, as they are often suggestive and make the viewer ponder imaginary scenarios (for example SLOW DRIVE by the bootleg boy 2 or Midnight Gazing by chilli music). These subtle invitations, as well as the overly supportive comment section— sometimes even to the extreme—create a safe space for these mesmerising moments.

Lofi for ghosts (only)
Homework Radio — 6 august 2019

The (fictional) nostalgia caused in the digital safe space of these videos can be seen as an escape from day-to-day society; a therapeutic happening where people find comfort in alternative universes of cosy rooms, late nights and rainy days. They are gateways to a scenario where we are relieved from the pressure of the future and of production. Instead, they radiate a sort of perpetual present where the urgencies of life have been suspended. In between the comments, we can explore a time of detachment from the commotions of the present. The threat, now, is no longer the deadly sweet seduction of nostalgia. The problem is no longer the longing to get back to the past, but the inability to get out of it. We end up in a grey-black drizzle of static, a haze of crackle, a micro-fiction that only occurs in our longing.

That makes me want to play Animal crossing.

God I miss those times. Playing Wild World late night.
School next day. Seeing my friends again.
Biggest problem being the homework I had to do.
Good days.

You check your phone again. 1:19 AM.
The light emanating from your cafe wallpaper strains
your eyes, but you push through the pain to open up
youtube. You search for this video, sit through another
obnoxious 15 second ad, and flip your phone over,
as you reach for your charger cable.

You just finished watching Your Name, and though you thought it was a beautiful story you can't help but feel a weight in your stomach press down harder than normal. Your relaxed face tenses up and your lip quivers. Tears begin to fall, streaming down the sides of your face, dampening your pillow.

It was a rough day. You didn't talk to anyone,
you sat through classes not taking notes, and you're
so mentally tired that the final math test of the semester
that you had been worrying about for weeks became
a nonfactor. It's already over, you never paid attention
and you never felt like studying. You just accept
the failure, the outrage from your parents, and that all
of your academic achievement throughout high school,
all the A's you earned, and emotionally poignant
college letters, have been for nothing. It's ok though,
you're comfortable now even if its just for a few hours.

The one relationship you had ended as quarantine
you began, and you think back to her and some
of the fun dates you went on, you remember that
you didn't even really like her, but that she was
your first girlfriend and that you had finally done it.
The tears come, faster now, from a light pitter-patter
on your pillow to a rhythmic dripping.

You think back to the protagonists of your name, and how everything worked out. Deep down in your heart of hearts you knew it would. But that's how fiction works.

You want to open your heart to the possibility
of connection, but it's been so many months since
real human interaction, you return to your old devices
and allow for your aching heart to settle to stone.
For a last time you think of that cafe you have
as your wallpaper. Even though its been three years
you still recall that quaint wooden structure,
bittersweet iced coffee, and relaxing odor of pine.

It is next summer you imagine meeting a lovely girl, and decide to show her the cafe. As the cicada's hum resonates throughout the melting sky you smile to yourself, and reach over. Her smooth hands clasp around yours as you walk up the hill. The golden rays of sun fade, leaving a fine portrait of purple and red hues in the sky. The old woman who still runs the shop greets you warmly, showing the both of you up to the balcony.

You and the girl both talk to each other, giggling and smiling. What you talked about wasn't important, but it was the best moment of your life. You wish this moment could last forever. The humming of the cicadas die down, and the sounds of the other customers, drinking their tea or coffee, chatting to friends, flipping through their books or typing on their computers becomes evident. You ask her if she wants to go, and leave a generous tip.

Before she goes you want to show her one last thing. There is a special spot down by the lake. You walk down the creaky wooden stairs of the cafe, exiting the door, and down the dark cobblestone steps. The only sounds now are the faint rustling of grass and the stepping of your feet. You tell her that the spot is really close and she blushes. After descending through to a band of conifers and narrow road, you stumble to the dock. The incandescent lanterns are aglow. You reach the end of the dock and pull her close, awkwardly pressing your lips into hers. She's slightly taken aback but leans into it almost pushing you over. You don't know what you're doing, but the only emotion running through your brain is pure happiness.

BEEP BEEP BEEP
your alarm blares. It is 8 AM.
Time for another day of school.

It was a nice dream and you wish it lasted longer.
You put it to paper to try and remember that dream
as best you can, but you can only put an incomplete
picture together. Surely you'll only jot down fragments
of the dream but it's the best you can do. It's time to flip
open your laptop and join the zoom call. You know
what struggles the day holds but armed with your nice
dream you feel just a little stronger. You kissed the girl,
and even if that kiss was just imaginary it gave
you the strength of an army.

It's ok. Push through it. Hold on to that dream like it's the last one of your life. You might just realize it. The japanese have a word for hope, called "kibo" きぼう. *Life is certainly not easy. In fact it is just about the hardest thing a person can go through. But have some* きぼう, *and maybe, just maybe your dream of that cafe will come true.*

POV: You're taking a trip to Japan for a few weeks
because it's been you're childhood dream for so long.
You & your all-time best friend are going together.
You're also going to celebrate you're 21st birthday
this year. You & you're friend arrive in the city
& decide to stay at the nice hotel for the trip.

It's going to be the clearest night of the whole year, so both of you sneak up to the hotel rooftop when security had left. You bring you're phones & astrology books with you to use on the rooftop. Once you open the door, you see almost a thousand stars lighting up the whole sky. You & your friend spend the night taking pictures, charting the constellations, playing your favorite songs, and reading all about the stars in your book.

As the sun starts to peak out from the edge of the horizon, your friend turns to you and says, "I hope you've had the best birthday of your life, and I hope we share this memory forever." "I'll always remember this night, thank you for making it so special." You & your friend hug eachother one last time & you walk back down to your hotel room to get some sleep. As you're lying down you appreciate the experience you've had & think to yourself, "I'm so grateful that I got to experience this crazy trip with my favorite person in the world."

You turn to your side to see your friend already asleep on the bed next to you. You smile & quietly whisper, "Love you."

*POV: Finals are finished and you decide to go on
a long drive with your childhood friends. You pack
the snacks and the other two bring stuffed animals,
a deck of cards, and flashlights with different colour
lenses. The three of you hop into the car and halfway
through, you drive on this bridge that gives the three
of you a heavenly view of a sparkling lake. You take
a deep breath, taking in all the feels: the roaring music
from late 2018, the smell of the fresh air mixed with
croissants from your snack stash, and the glimmering
lake that you may-or-may-not ever see again.
Life is just fine*

To relax/ study & retrospecting capitalism

That small intermezzo of emotionally (sometimes over-) charged micro-fictions is the perfect gateway to cross over into why these commenters might long for a different time with less responsibility and fewer worries.

I do not intend to state that we all take a trip down memory lane while listening to lo-fi, not at all actually. When we look at the live chat that accompanies these streams, we are often confronted with people talking about their workload. People discussing their homework or an upcoming deadline are often met with encouraging and supportive comments that *they can do it, they can go that extra mile.*

From this, it should be no stretch to say that we are aware that the genre of lo-fi hip hop can have a positive influence on our focus and our ability to stay productive.

Well, it's 4AM and you're still studying.
Your getting things done, and if no one has told you yet,
I'm proud of you.

*Post-fordism,
revolution or
devolution*

Side B

It is not a coincidence that these streams go on 24/7. As we are producing, studying or working with lo-fi hip hop in the background, we are confronted by the fact that our society has changed drastically. The terms coined for this change, from Fordist capitalism to Post-Fordist capitalism, finds its origin with French Marxist and American philosophers in the 70s and 80s and to this day still has some form of ambiguity to it. Post-Fordism is briefly brought into the context of the lo-fi community by Emma Winston in her *Beats to Study/Relax To: Contradiction and Paradox in Lo-Fi Hip Hop*. Through this essay, we will define Post-Fordism as an economic model of work following the revolution caused by the automation of the labour market. It evolved from a Fordist system where everything was seen as a system of mass production, and thus mass consumerism existed alongside it. Everything was standardised, a famous quote from Henry Ford even said that "they can have any color car, as long as it's black." Yet, presumably, the Fordist age started crumbling in the 70s due to multiple reasons: the rise of the computer and a need for smaller multi-skilled workforces being two of the more prominent ones. Instead of mass production focused on the masses, it started to shift towards specific groups and subcultures. And vice versa, consumers could now start to adapt products to their personal tastes.

This had a huge impact on the workforce. A large number of semi-skilled workers that were manning simplistic machinery suddenly found themselves to be obsolete.

In Post-Fordist capitalism, 'affective labour' is foregrounded. Affective labour is a market that focuses on communication, emotion and intellect, as theorist Paolo Virno states:

In the Post-Fordist environment, a decisive role is played by the infinite variety of concepts and logical schemes which cannot ever be set within fixed capital, being inseparable from the reiteration of a plurality of living subjects. The general intellect includes, thus, formal and informal knowledge, imagination, ethical propensities, mindsets, and 'linguistic games'.

[...]

The general intellect becomes an attribute of living labor when the activity of the latter consists increasingly of linguistic services.

A GRAMMAR OF THE MULTITUDE: FOR AN ANALYSIS OF CONTEMPORARY FORMS OF LIFE, Paulo Virno (2004), p. 107-108.

What we can deduce from this small excerpt is that the Fordist economy was a rigid system for the worker and their set of tasks that was clear. The Post-Fordist system is a confusing state for this worker; there are infinitely more tasks to fulfil in the desire for adaptability that rules individualistic consumerism and it demands a tremendous emotional and personal investment from the worker to stay up to date with the demands of work. Post-Fordism has been a phenomenon in development since the 70s and is developing now faster than ever before because of the advancements in technology. We are now met with generations growing up without knowing anything else. Nowadays, work is related to emotion, as we are being told that we are a producing-desire machine and it is inherent to being human, according to Deleuze and Guattari in *Anti-Œdipus*. The two elaborate on the premise of humans

and the embedded need to produce, not
as a contemporary thing, but a universal primary
process. Lo-fi music, as a product of this recent
development in capitalism, plays with some
of these aspects of desire to produce, 'Beats
to work to' so to say. Yet what Emma Winston
states to be so significant in her academic essay
on the paradoxical layers of lo-fi, is that the
listener is born in this time of Post-Fordism,
where this pressure and responsibility
to produce and participate has always existed.

24/7 in the background

Waiting on the train, I am surrounded by people
who have shut themselves off from the world. It's early
in the morning and I scroll on YouTube, finding
a tracklist in my suggestion called Morning Coffee
Chillhop. *A small loop of a cup of coffee and its heat*
is shown on the thumbnail. Thirty-three minutes.
An excellent amount of time for breakfast. Yet I had
to rush through the cold. Luckily I was able to let
it play throughout the commute, even without
a reflective cup of coffee to go along with these
chillhop beats as I enjoyed the moment in my mind.

The context of Post-Fordism and pressure of current-day capitalism in which lo-fi exists, mirrors the chapter that discussed melancholy. It tunes in to the idea of production and that seems quite a stretch from thinking about childhood times. Josef Pieper, a German philosopher, discussed this idea in one of his essays dating back to 1952 on Charles Baudelaire, a French 19th century Symbolist poet and art critic.

LEISURE, THE BASIS OF CULTURE, Josef Pieper (2015), p. 77.

"The vacancy left by absence of worship is filled by mere killing of time and by boredom, which is directly related to inability to enjoy leisure; for one can only be bored if the spiritual power to be leisurely has been lost. There is an entry in Baudelaire... "One must work, if not from taste then at least from despair. For, to reduce everything to a single truth: work is less boring than pleasure."

Pieper continues that we can not "acquiesce to being", and that we "overwork as a means of self-escape, as a way of trying to justify our existence."

This little piece by Pieper is written in a Fordist society. We can assume that, even when people went to work to turn away from self-reflection, most of them still went home in the evening without lingering worries about work because there was less of an emotional engagement. This was still during the years of financial growth and the accompanying carelessness concerning conditions of living. Pieper was writing during that same time, but since then we have only strayed further away from the self-reflection that is critical for us as human beings. Now, confronted with the idea of the Post-Fordist expectation of constant production and the responsibility that is demanded by the current-day capitalist overhead, there is very little space for emotional commitment besides work. Lo-fi listeners are working with their headphones on, in a cocoon, sheltered from the outside world so they can stay focused on their studying and their work.

Blade Runner 2049: Dream-engineer Ana works while she is talking and promises she will hear every word K says while doing so. 'Lo-fi beats to study to' and Post-Fordism suggest that we are forced into a condition of producing whilst doing multiple other activities at the same time, be it relaxing, listening to music, conversing with others. Ana is aware of her surroundings, capable of listening to K, creating birthday memories for a stranger at the same time.

More and more, listeners of the genre are pushing themselves harder, and the supportive chat to the right side of the video aids this idea of continuing to produce. There is no break in the live-stream. One has the option to implement ads for revenue in their compilations of lo-fi, yet when there is a live stream—the most well-known stream is on the YouTube channel LoFi girl—there are no ads interrupting this. It would be awkward if an ad suddenly pops up, only to break the productive trance you're in. It just keeps playing, 24/7. Although lo-fi originated in the virtual world of SoundCloud and YouTube, we can now often find links to Spotify playlists.

There is a playlist of lo-fi music created by Spotify, a music application that tunes into this never-ending playing of sound and music.

They try to infiltrate consumers' everyday life, for as long as possible, advertising music to play at work, at home, whilst on a run and so on. Lo-fi seems to be a great genre for this, as it embodies certain characteristics of non-listening, non-entertaining music. A genre that exists with a single purpose: to fill the background.

This idea of background music is not new. Erik Satie, a French composer, coined the term 'furniture music' in 1917. In French, it is 'mystique d'ameublement', which actually leans more into furnishing music, opposed to furniture. Short, repetitive classical pieces that were played on repeat for an indefinite amount of time, thereby blending into the background of the scene people find themselves in. 'Elevator music' is my favourite contemporary example of this: it is only there to create a mood to accompany the limbo state while standing in an elevator with strangers. Its purpose is clearing the setting of —what is often interpreted as— the awkward silence. Yet, if we listen to Satie's classical pieces or elevator music these days, we are aware of it playing, as it is not up to date with our current music scene. Lo-fi tracks, just like furniture music, flow into each other and it is not always easy to distinguish when one track ends and a new one starts. Thus they become a perfect, present-day setlist for a never-ending stream that plays in the background of the listener's everyday life.

*The hyper-real
companion*

As she pets her cat, one can imagine petting a cat oneself. She looks up through the window to catch a glimpse of the outside world, we look up towards our screen to catch a glimpse of an idealised world.

The most popular stream (now LoFi girl) used to be by ChilledCow (the same person, although the account ended up being suspended for using a copyrighted image by Studio Ghibli's *Whisper of the Heart*). That stream went on for a consecutive 13.165 hours before it got interrupted. 13.000 hours of a looped animation where a girl is seated in a perpetual streak of studying. She turns the pages of a seemingly endless book that seems to contain some theory to be studied.

Even the commenters notice this comical aspect of the Sisyphean lo-fi girl; a loop that is only a couple of seconds long, emphasising a ceaseless pile of books to be studied and work to be done.

*Mimicking
an animation*

The Sisyphean lo-fi girl becomes the companion of the listener, whom they can always count on. In this way, she becomes a partner-in-work and to some, an emotionally loaded image that relates to late nights of work behind their own desk. The listener has come to the point that they choose to ignore the outside world, only to reside in the world of production accompanied by an animated companion. In that way, studying lo-fi music might be in line with what Baudrillard says, late 20th century critical theorist, who heavily leans into the concepts of postmodernism and symbolism exchange. He wrote on the hyper-real, a semiotic term about *the generation of models of a real without origin or reality* (Baudrillard, *Simulacra and Simulation*). Hyper-reality is a representation without an original referent. Something that refers to an act or image, yet the image does not exist in our reality, for example Santa Claus. Even though it does not come from an existing reality, it feels real because our consciousness is unable to distinguish reality from the simulation of reality.

A concrete 'more than real' example is a hamburger. When we desire a burger, or even enjoy a real one, the cause of desire and pleasure isn't the physical burger (this is merely a case of semiotics, Baudrillard does not deny the burger's existence). But the burger from a commercial, the one that looks better than any real burger may ever be, is the image we imagine to consume. For Baudrillard, this is how the fantasy and fictional image rules over our everyday life. The perfect burger appears real, but is actually hyper-real, as it is built on layers of subconscious signification. All of those layers make our plain hamburger, the much less exciting "real" real hamburger, redundant.

The fantasy ends up infesting whatever traces of reality there are. In lo-fi, we are studying to an image that encourages the idea of studying, the lo-fi girl and other illustrative derivatives. This image is related to the hyper-real in the sense that it shows a scenario that is purely fictional yet is elevated to a happening we long for. I might even call the animation a never-ending loop that idealises this event that is being part of production. We are studying along with the 'lo-fi girl', trying to focus on our tasks with a live chat and a community supporting us. She becomes an icon, even an idol, who encourages us to be like her, to be in the zone of studying or working. She encourages us to relax, whilst actually being productive, as the title puts the terms of relaxation and production next to each other as equals. We study and place ourselves in her shoes, because she is a major example of peak productivity. Instead of imagining the better hamburger, we play lo-fi in the background and imagine ourselves looking like the perpetual drawn animation of someone who is endlessly at work in what could be called a perfect work-environment. Petting that cat in what takes only a second of the animated loop, is the only break she takes from the endless bundle of paper of what we can think is a notebook filled with theory. In this idealisation of what would be an everlasting production (as it is a 24/7 stream) of studying/working, she ends up being a model of today's Post-Fordist society. She is bound to her studying, trapped in a loop of time that of the animator's choice. Just as we are trapped in a cycle of adding to the system of production.

*Optimising
relaxation*

Calm Your Stress
Neotic —21 april 2021

Calm your Stress *by Neotic. Lisa Simpson in the void*
of the universe. An abstract cube surrounds her as
a light box. The implication of the title sets the mood.
A troublesome day with some setbacks results in me
sitting on the floor, shrouded by the sound from
my headphones. I am glad the day has almost come
to an end and commit myself to relaxing, trying
to achieve a similar state to the one of Lisa meditating
with an older generation iPod as her only companion,

Thirty-four minutes have passed by quickly, I probably
lost myself in a comparable mental void.

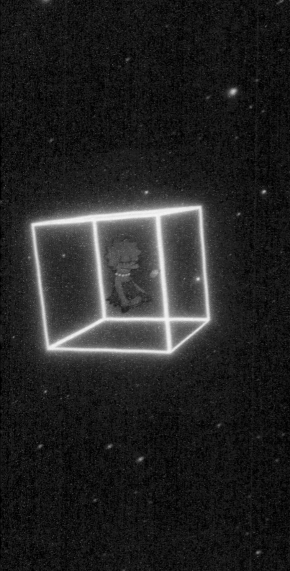

Working while being accompanied by a looped animation of a cartoon, by non-distracting music, can be useful. Although this music has a clear layer of induced emotions, it has been hijacked as a tool for optimal productivity, and when the work is finished, it remains playing in the background, though now as a way of winding down and relaxing. That is assuming that it is even possible to wind down from work in today's society, as work and worries of non-producing linger on endlessly in the back of our minds. We are no longer used to doing nothing and take offence at being passive. We tell ourselves we must always be working, reading or contributing to society. We must go out and spend our earnings, be social and consume.

Theodor Adorno is a mid-twentieth century writer, who, same as Walter Benjamin, was part of the Frankfurter Schule. He focused on the subjects of critical theory, psychoanalysis, art critique, and socialist beliefs. Adorno wrote about the difference between 'free time' and 'leisure time' and how we are indoctrinated to either spend money or work to produce money in today's society. Adorno differentiates between two kinds of free time. 'Leisure time' saw its origin in the twentieth century and is often related to hobbies or going out. He writes that leisure time often suggests that you have to consume, to buy and thus contribute to the economy. Examples of this are hobbies like cycling, that nudge you towards buying a bike, or upgrading your bike to be able to cycle easier. Yet 'leisure time' can also be seen as a social act where we go out with friends to a restaurant or bar, where we consume for the entire evening. Opposed to that, we have 'free time'. Free time is where we do nothing, or something that doesn't require spending any money like walking (excluding high-tier walking shoes or the idea that we have to travel towards faraway places to walk).

'Free time' is where we do nothing but being in the present is essential to humanity. It is a discouraging development that we are now placing the term 'relaxing' as an equal to the terms of 'studying/producing'. It is also disconcerting that music and emotionally-charged samples of popular culture are reduced, denigrated and dismissed as a tool for production, something that exists only in the background. As addressed before, background music is nothing new, yet is used in non-spaces. Non-spaces are places where one is forced to wait and be passive, like an elevator or waiting room. Lo-fi music —and other background music like elevator music that is found playing in the background of these non-spaces— has become a valuable way to support focus and concentration a little more.

This 24/7 phenomenon of work and relaxation combined, adds to the stress and burnout culture ruling contemporary society. It is no surprise that we see an almost hyperbolical rise of exhaustion in today's millennial-burnout culture. We end up relaxing with the same music that keeps us focusing on work. One could even say we should focus on relaxing as much as we focus on working. The sooner we feel relaxed (which I believe is an almost impossible task with today's endless list of worries), the sooner we can go back to producing. It can be compared to the settings of a room's air-conditioning, where one puts the temperature on the setting that ends up stimulating people to work longer and more attentively.

*Comforting
adblock*

As the stream starts, I click on the inescapable ad,
knowing that once the live-stream is playing I will
be submerged in a lo-fi scene, accompanied by
my hyper-real companions on loop. I don't have
to worry about screeching ads that elaborate on
clever investments of dropshipping, interrupting
my listening session.

Like a curator of a museum, LoFi Girl walks
me through a soundscape of beats to which
I can relax/study.

Not everything contributes to the everlasting loop of capitalist production. In the shadows of big corporations and our dominating Post-Fordist society that encourages us to never rest, the lo-fi community can only exist through platforms of YouTube, SoundCloud, TikTok ads etc. Yet in these digital environments where work and advertising have crept up in what used to be our free time and time for relaxation, we see small attempts of protest and resistance.

First off, there is the fact that lo-fi is often collected into a playlist, also called a mix that lasts longer than a couple of tracks. We find carefully human-curated playlists on YouTube that set a specific mood, be it sad, relaxed or downtempo. Yet, this also goes against an aspect that is key to the revenue of YouTube, namely the algorithm that pushes us to watch the next recommended video and so we often watch the accompanied ad as well, which we can only skip after 5 seconds. Besides that the ad would disrupt our possible focus and thus damage our production, we are confronted with a painful reminder of consumerism. Of course, this chapter is only correct in case we don't have an extension like AdBlock installed in our browser. A person curates these tracks into a playlist and then chooses to rebel against the corporation to limit their possible ad revenue, a small act of aggression, yet a meaningful one. Then again, this needs nuance as some playlists of an hour do implement ads throughout the video for the same revenue.

*Digital
psychoanalyst*

These traits of the lo-fi community creates
a contemporary, digital space relatable
to the feeling one would have walking
into a psychologist's practice, where
there is a chaise longue accompanied
by bookshelves filled with Freud,
Lacan and so on.

The 24/7 chat that accompanies the
livestream with wholesome messages of support
and the comments below the video that are filled
with, micro-fictions and encouraging phrases
to cheer the listener on, create a possibility
to connect to other people.

ISTARI
1 MONTH AGO

*studying doesn't always go the way we want it to,
but as long as we each have a few chill lofi beats
at 12 a.m., we can do it.*

ARNAV UPAD-
HYAY
5 MONTHS AGO

*To everyone who's studying with this music:
After an hour, you should stand up and walk a bit
around. Better stop the music or put on different music
for the break. Open your window, even if it's cold
outside. Fresh air will make it better, trust me. [...]*

Using these common examples, we could state
that the community is almost uncharacteristically
friendly. Listeners struggling to keep up with their
everlasting workload from school or work, others
who are battling possible loneliness or listeners
who carry a mental burden on their shoulders,
are met with open arms and comfort. Everyone
seems to support each other in this struggle. Besides
being comforted, it is also an easy way for people
to connect. As the chat fills with people who love
or at least appreciate lo-fi music, they are drawn
to the wholesome interactions that take place
in the chat or comment section. "I had a rough
day" can be met with "We're here for you,
tomorrow is a new opportunity." All this takes
place on platforms that are governed by a capitalist
corporation, and is hijacked to support people
who might be struggling because of that.
In resistance, we find an anonymous, digital space
where people are encouraged by the community

to write down their worries. This is not just because of the chat and comments, but the first impression is often found in the phrasing of the title, which immediately constructs a mood. Now, this is not the case with all lo-fi mixes and I think we have to note that this is a specific subgenre of the community that really starts to lean into the moody, more doomer-type aspect of the soundscape. Nevertheless, the fact that these wholesome communities are able to exist on large platforms, that are often built upon algorithms chasing profits, is an amazing feat that stresses the importance of the virtual therapeutic place they construct.

Emma Winston states that even the online lo-fi environment inevitably tumbled into a 'control society', a term coined by Gilles Deleuze, French critical theorist and philosopher of the late 20th century. He writes that before the control society came the discipline society, which was defined by discrete, physical barriers such as schools, office buildings and industry. A control society reaches beyond these easily defined, institutionally regulated places and influences the individual throughout their entire life. This control society is able to follow us everywhere, even into our bedroom where they are able to check our phone usage late at night. Yet the lo-fi community plays with this in a subtle, yet clear way. The users are anonymous and there are consequence-free interactions between strangers that allows a subspace to exist. In this subspace, the control society can still track our activity, yet we, as users, are distracted. We are able to temporarily escape from what the post-Fordist market wants us to do.

John Newton
@playthatjohn

If you recognize this girl you're either:

A.) Being productive
B.) Being unproductive
C.) Going through some shit
D.) All of the above

*Time to close
my laptop*

A defining aspect of the age we live
in is the complete destruction of the uncanny.
Where we used to experience feelings of mysticism
and unease, we now experience a shift of dullness
caused by our awareness. The hi-fi music we started
out with is a great example. We have replaced
the unheimlich tingle of unknowingness with
a knowingness and a hyper-awareness. We do
not give any space to ambiguous existence, nothing
is left undefined. Lo-fi, by contrast to this postmodern tendency, is a context of the half-forgotten,
poorly remembered and the vague emotional state
we acquire when looking back on a past without
the worries created by that same postmodern society.

Being immersed in both the imagined
and the real at once, seems an appropriate way
to engage with a reality. A reality where impossible
expectations are quintessential to defining ordinary
life. The vague overlap between fantasy and reality
might construct this alternate plane, where one
can barely escape the grasp of Post-Fordism and
the control society that goes hand in hand with it.

In this momentary illusion, there is peace.
This peace might be based on a group of anonymous
people you can vent your worries to, or it may
be based on memories, even if they never occurred
in reality. A livestream with 1000 viewers from
across the world loops. Some of these viewers must
be on their way in a daily commute, some probably
working late into the night. Yet the one thing
that connects them is this digitally curated form
of lo-fi escape.

This small collection of connections related to lo-fi music is merely an attempt at me mapping the nostalgia that seems to rule this current day and age. It is an assumption, but this carefully curated lo-fi community is an intrinsic attempt to transcend the pressure weighing down on a generation.

Bibliography

'The life and death of media' in *Sound Unbound*, Bruce Sterling (2008), page 76.

The Chase - *Avatar: The Last Airbender, Book 2* (2006).

Anti-Climacus in the Sickness unto Death, Soren Kierkegaard (2004), page 176-177.

'Postmodernism and Consumer Society' in *The Cultural Turn: Selected writings on the Postmodern*, Fredric Jameson (1983-1998), Verso, 1998, page 8.

Ghosts of My Life: Writings on Depression, Hauntology and Lost Futures, Mark Fisher (2014).

Beats to Relax/Study To: Contradiction and Paradox in Lofi Hip Hop, Emma Winston, IASPM Journal (January 2019).

The Future of Nostalgia, Svetlana Boym (2002).

Blade Runner 2049, Denis Villeneuve (2017).

Illuminations, Walter Benjamin (1968), ed. Hannah Arendt.

Berlin Childhood (revised in 1938), Walter Benjamin (2006).

A Grammar of the Multitude: For an Analysis of Contemporary Forms of Life, Paul Virno (2004), page 107-108.

https://infed.org/post-modernism-and-post-modernity/ (consulted on 12 august 2021).

https://www.newyorker.com/culture/cultural-comment/against-chill-apathetic-music-to-make-spreadsheets-to (consulted on 8 september 2021).

Simulacra and Simulation, Jean Baudrillard (1995).

Free Time in The Culture Industry – *Selected Essays on Mass Culture*, Theodor W. Adorno (2001), Routledge.

Civilization and its discontents, Sigmund Freud, (1930).

Leisure, the Basis of Culture, Josef Pieper, p. 77 (2015).

Videography

lofi hip hop radio –
beats to relax/study to
Lofi Girl. Ongoing originally
Studio Ghibli's Shizuku
Tsukishima from the film:
Whisper of the Heart [3],
revisited by Juan Pablo
Machado.

SOUL SEARCHING²
Neotic, 31 august 2020.
Artwork created by Matt
Groening, owned by 20th
Television Animation.

SOUL SEARCHING³
Neotic, 21 march 2021.
Artwork created by Matt
Groening, owned by 20th
Television Animation.

You're in Hey Arnold's room
in 1997 listening to music
and it's raining | 3 HOUR
ASMR Ambience
Kitspy's Dreamland,
28 june 2021. Created
by Craig Bartlett. Owned
by Nickelodeon Animation
Studio.

1 HR Uncle Iroh Inspiration |
Avatar Lofi Study Beats
Olivia Tatara,
29 december 2019.

the mandalorian – lofi.
Closed on Sunday,
2 november 2020. Artist
unknown. The mandalorian
owned by Disney.

SLOW DRIVE
the bootleg boy 2,
2 april 2021.

Midnight Gazing – Lofi hip hop
mix – Stress Relief, Relaxing Music
chilli music, 26 may 2021.
Artwork created by Matt
Groening, owned by 20th
Television Animation.

Lo-fi for Ghosts (Only)
Homework Radio, 6 august
2019. Artwork created
by Wren @sleeprealms –
http://sleeprealms.tumblr.com/

Calm Your Stress
Neotic, 12 april 2021.
Artwork created by Matt
Groening, owned by 20th
Television Animation.

Morning Coffee Chillhop.
Lo Fi Electronic Mix
Lin Zhiyi, 28 november 2017.

Colophon

Longing For Lo-Fi
Onomatopee 248

ISBN: 978-94-93148-97-0
Author: Sébastien Bovie

Graphic design: Lisa Ladent
Editors: Tseu Ying Tang,
Jesse Muller, Natasha Rijkhoff
Proofreader: Silvana
Gordon Valenzuela

Typeface:
ABC Gaisyr by Dinamo,
designed by Fabian Harb,
Michelangelo Nigra
Spacing and Kerning:
Igino Marini.
Apple SD Gothic Neo by
Sandoll Communications Inc.

Printing: Printon

Paper inside:
Munken Lynx Rough 90g/m^2
Paper cover:
Munken Lynx 300g/m^2

Published by Onomatopee
Projects, Eindhoven NL
Jesse Muller &
Natasha Rijkhoff

First Edition 2023.